HANUKKAH, HERE I COME!

For Daniel, Micah, and Noah—DJS

GROSSET & DUNLAP
An Imprint of Penguin Random House LLC, New York

Penguin supports copyright. Copyright fuels creativity, encourages diverse voices, promotes free speech,
and creates a vibrant culture. Thank you for buying an authorized edition of this book and for complying with
copyright laws by not reproducing, scanning, or distributing any part of it in any form without permission.
You are supporting writers and allowing Penguin to continue to publish books for every reader.

Text copyright © 2021 by David Steinberg. Illustrations copyright © 2021 by Sara Palacios.
All rights reserved. Published by Grosset & Dunlap, an imprint of Penguin Random House LLC, New York.
GROSSET & DUNLAP is a registered trademark of Penguin Random House LLC.
Manufactured in China.

Visit us online at www.penguinrandomhouse.com.

Library of Congress Cataloging-in-Publication Data is available upon request.

ISBN 9780593094266   10 9 8 7 6 5 4 3 2 1

HANUKKAH,
HERE I COME!

BY D. J. STEINBERG
ILLUSTRATED BY SARA PALACIOS

GROSSET & DUNLAP

HANUKKAH, HERE I COME!
The sun's sinking fast. The candles are set.
The presents are stacked. (Which one will I get?!)

Something good in the kitchen
makes the whole house smell *yum*.
The holiday's starting . . .
Hanukkah, here I come!

MACCA-BAM! MACCA-BOOM!

There was a brave young hero
named Judah Maccabee.
Macca-*BAM!* Macca-*BOOM!*
That Maccabee made history!

With his band of Macca-brothers,
he fought to save the day—
Macca-*BAM!* Macca-*BOOM!*
The bad guys ran away!

The Jews took back their Temple and lit the holy lights.
Just a little bit of oil lasted eight whole days and nights.
And that is what we celebrate on Hanukkah each year—
Macca-*BAM!* Macca-*BOOM!*
Give a Judah Macca-*CHEER!*

THE SHAMMES

One-two-three-four-five-six-seven-eight.
A candle for each night we celebrate!
But let's not forget about candle nine.
The shammes helps all the other eight shine!

THE FIRST NIGHT OF HANUKKAH

Gather round the window to light the very first light.
We sing the Hanukkah blessings to welcome the very first night.
Other windows down the street flicker into view,
as other families gather round their front windows, too!

WHAT'S INSIDE?

What's inside my Hanukkah box?
Oh, pretty please—don't let it be socks!
Hope you're not bunny slippers or a robe to enjoy.
When I open you up,
pretty please—be a TOY!

ALL WRAPPED UP!

I love to wrap presents for everyone!
I have a wrapping habit.
I wrapped eight carrots with eight little bows
and a Hanukkah card for my rabbit!

HANUKKAH SELFIES

Everyone pose by the candles!
Look at the camera and smile.
We'll all remember this Hanukkah
in good old selfie style!

Click! That one cut off my sister.
Click! Where's my mother's head?
Click! That one's dark and blurry.
Click! That's Mom's finger instead.

We snap a dozen pictures,
and they all cut someone in half.
We'll all remember this Hanukkah
when we look at the selfies and laugh!

CHOCOLATE GELT

Gelt are special Hanukkah coins,
and no other coins can beat 'em,
'cause they're the only kind in the world
that you can unwrap and eat 'em!

GIMME A GIMEL!

Spinning dreidel spinning free,
which Hebrew letter will it be?
Whirl-twirl spinning top,
slowly, s l o w l y to a stop.
Please, not shin or nun or hay.
Gimme a gimel to win the day!

HOW TO PLAY DREIDEL

Put your gelt on the table.
Player one spins the dreidel . . .

נ Nun, you get nothing.

ש Shin, put one in.

ה Hay, you take half.

ג Get a gimel—you win!

DIZZY DREIDELS

My sister and I spin like dreidels
until we fall down on the ground,
but even when we stop spinning,
the whole house keeps spinning around!

WE'RE HERE!

We made it to Bubbe and Grandpa's.
We leap up the steps to the door.

Bubbe squishes us in her soft arms
and scoops us off the floor.

Grandpa twirls us high in the air—
he makes us laugh and shriek—
then pulls us in for a kiss attack,
cheek to scratchy cheek!

A FAVOR FOR MY GRANDPA

Bubbe fries the latkes.
Grandpa puts them on a platter.
"Oh no!" he calls to me.
I say, "Grandpa, what's the matter?"
"We cannot serve this latke!"
He gives it a good poke.

SOUR CREAM

APPLE SAUCE

"Why not?" I ask. He lifts it up.
"Well, look at it. It broke!
What a terrible disaster!
I really hate to waste it,
but I guess I'll throw it out, unless . . .
perhaps *you* want to taste it?"

23

"I do!" I grab that latke.
It's so full of crispy flavor.
"Thanks a million." Grandpa winks.
"You sure did me a favor!"

APPLESAUCE VS. SOUR CREAM

When you eat a latke,
you must pick a team:
Are you on Team Applesauce
or Team Sour Cream?

It's an age-old dispute
that goes on to this day.
Applesauce? Sour cream?
What do you have to say?

CAN'T HEAR YOU!

When my family all gets together,
we're a pretty rowdy crowd.
Everyone likes to talk at once,
so the house can get kind of loud.
I think the whole world can hear us,
from Buffalo to Boise—
What's that? Did you say something?
Couldn't hear you, 'cause it's *WAY TOO NOISY*!!

ENOUGH FOOD?

My grandparents always worry,
"Will there be enough to eat?"

They cooked and cooked and cooked so much,
I think they could feed the whole street!

A JELLY DOUGHNUT WARNING

Beware!
Jelly doughnuts are dangerous.
They squirt when you take a bite!
And *poof*!
That powdered sugar explodes
and turns your face all white!

THE LAST NIGHT OF HANUKKAH

The candle box is empty.
Eight candles are burning low.
It's the last night of Hanukkah.
Where did the time all go?
We watch the candles sputter out
from our couch, all warm and snug.
And then Mom and Dad pull us closer . . .

for one last Hanukkah hug.